A Spider Walked

By

Brielle Bartel
Illustrations

ISBN:1-7345709-0-8

ISBN-13:978-1-7345709-0-8

First Edition 2020
10 9 8 7 6 5 4 3 2 1

No spiders were harmed in the making of this story.
Tim the cat wishes you well.
Ned, Clarence and dust bunny Fred are waiting inside,
and gold fishy too.

*For
Elliana*

In memory of Traci

The journey starts on the next page.

Or the next one.

A spider walked by as I sat on my bed.

A spider walked by and almost sat on my head.

My room is small and I am too.

I'm called Ruthie Jane, to some it seems plain,

but my daddy and mum call me R-J;

I prefer Ruthie Jane.

Days turn into weeks, as the spider walked by,

suspended from the ceiling, on a thread of silky
web.

He is the last thing I see, when my daddy tucks
me in,

and the first thing I notice when I

rub the sleep crackles from my eyes.

I've named him Clarence.

Clarence the spider to be exact.

I think he is a nice spider, as a matter of fact.

My fluffy stuffed bear sits next to me in bed,

where he gives me hugs and I tug at his head.

He is brown with black eyes and a red ribbon
around his neck.

I've tugged him so hard he is surely a wreck!

His neck is thinner now and stuffing not thick.

I sure hope Clarence does not land on his head;

that would be a fright while I am sitting in bed.

Summer turns to fall and all the leaves go brown—

the swimming pool downtown is all but shutdown.

I was playing there this summer when the sun was so warm

and the freckles on my nose appeared like a swarm.

I ran home from school that very first day of fall—

and burst through the door to look up at the wall.

Clarence was bouncing in his web gleefully,

perched above him a gift, it was a flea, that barely I could see.

They ran in circles across the spindly web, searching for each other—

oh I think that flea may be DEAD!

A spider you see is a creature not unlike you or me.

They must have something to eat or perish and that would not be neat.

I sure hope he doesn't eat that flea in front of me.

I'm kind of squeamish when it comes to eating, SUSHI!

Clarence frolics about as he jumps on his web.

Spinning a cocoon far above my head.

The flea has disappeared inside the silky spread,

asleep for awhile I assume, as I scratch my head.

My fiery red hair falls below my shoulders

with long locks and twisty curls that I
continuously brush.

Sometimes when I get angry my face turns red
as I blush.

Wintry snow falls outside my bedroom window.

Where neighborhood kids have turned the street into a slippery slope.

I hope Tommy Turner falls on his butt.

He laughs as he plays, taunting the other kids on the street.

He thinks he is so funny and his feet so complete.

The icy road is barren, the cars put to bed.

I wish I could play too, except for the cold in my head.

My nose it runs faster than I am able to catch.

A sniffle comes often as I watch my friends play.

I wish I was outside with them where I could play.

It is not fair that I am stuck inside today.

Under my bed lives a dust bunny named Fred.

He shoots back and forth when I blow on his head.

I stretch my neck as I lean over the edge.

Looking for my friend, dust bunny Fred.

Fred grows bigger and bigger under my bed.

He is dusty and hairy and that's why I call him Fred.

He looks like my uncle who has no hair on his head.

My uncle has bushy ears, just like dear old Fred.

Fred bounces across the floor, escaping the clutches of Ted.

We named our vacuum after our dog who lives in Club Med.

Ted sucks and slurps the dust off the floor—into its bowels where it is seen no more.

A light on the front shimmers and shakes—you better watch out Fred, I think Ted has lost his brakes.

As Fred scurries ahead and out of its wrath.

Fred can run fast when the vacuum comes past.

He shoots to the back of the bed and huddles as it zooms by.

The vacuum leaves my room and will not return soon.

Fred is happy to be alone under the bed away from certain doom.

There are no monsters under my bed.

Just a hairy friend—

called dust bunny Fred.

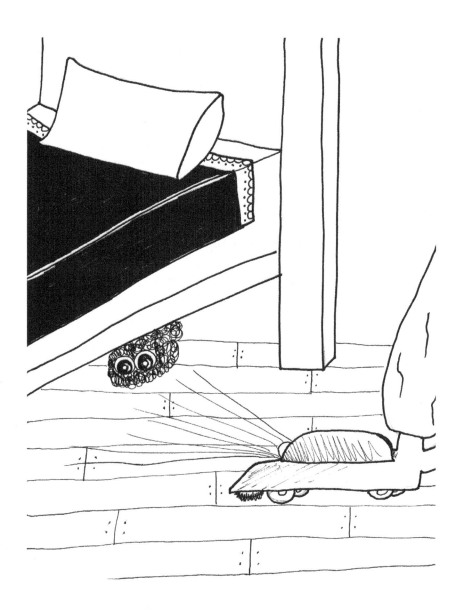

A raven squawks loud outside my front door.

I shot out of bed and ran up to the window to explore.

I press my nose up against the glass—hot breath makes fog as I steam up the glass.

I have to be quiet this Saturday morn',

or hear the wrath of my parents scorn.

It is too early for a little girl with red hair.

I better keep quiet as I search from my chair.

I rock back and forth with nary a squeak—

as I search the tree outside and look for a beak.

The raven squawks over and over to the giggles of me.

I can't spot him yet, oh dang, now I have to pee.

I run out of the bathroom as fast as can be—

to search for the raven I surely should see.

He's sitting qworking and squawking and qworking you see,

but a limb is blocking him from me.

The tree is spindly and icy as can be.

Winter has gripped this tree right in front of me.

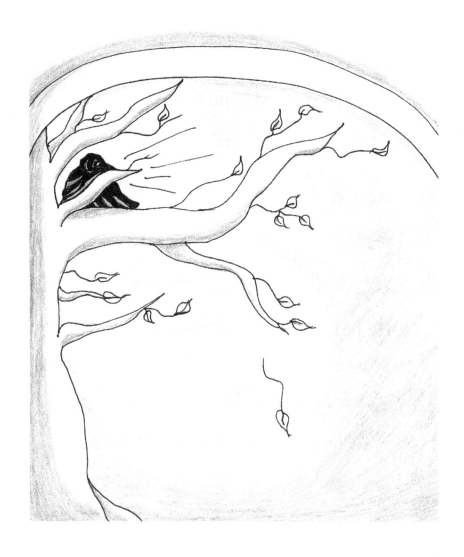

Time will tell if the raven I see.

Maybe he will leave that tree for me.

A wing flaps hard and I can see.

A feather falls off and out of that tree.

He shudders and shimmers and shimmies in
front of me,

that black bird has stood up and walked over to
me.

I open the window and a cold breeze blows in.

That raven is bold and walks onto my hand.

He has joined my bedroom fairy land.

With Clarence and Fred and a raven named Ned.

My world is complete so you see as I do.

I better not tell daddy or my mummy too.

My front tooth aches in my head want to see?

I pull on it hard but it does not come free.

My mum says it is old and a new one will come.

But first I must wait and I cannot chew gum.

For days it twists to the left and back to the right.

My tongue is in a battle with that tooth and it does not feel right.

A twelve round exhibition. It is a prize title fight!

My daddy comes home from work and cups my face to see—

if that tooth has broke loose or is not quite free.

He pushes gently with a finger on it.

I wince with pain and down I sit.

He says, "don't worry, it will come free.

Life is a bit slow, as you will see.

If you just have patience the tooth will come free."

He gives me a smile and then he adds,

"If you lose that tooth tonight, I will be a happy dad."

For teeth are worth money that much I can see.

Five dollars the tooth fairy will give to me.

My daddy says that is too much for me.

I think not, life is not free.

My cat sits curled up at my feet on my bed,

where Ted, Ned and Clarence stare at his head.

Let's not forget—dust bunny Fred.

We call him Tim, yes, that is my cat. He is a bit chubby and you might call him fat!

He is so content to sleep at my feet.

I am under my covers and under a sheet.

My nose peeks out from time to time.

To see if Tim is sleeping. Oh yes! Tim the cat is just fine.

Tim snorts and snores and wheezes a bit,

as he stretches his paws and kicks at my feet.

We battle for dominance over my bed,

where Ted and Ned and a spider named
Clarence sits overhead.

Tim the cat is lazy, I won't tell.

I have to yell twice when I ring his dinner bell.

For now he is asleep, next to my feet,

and all is well in my bed—

wait I forgot about dust bunny Fred, who is
under my bed and

the raven who sleeps next to my head.

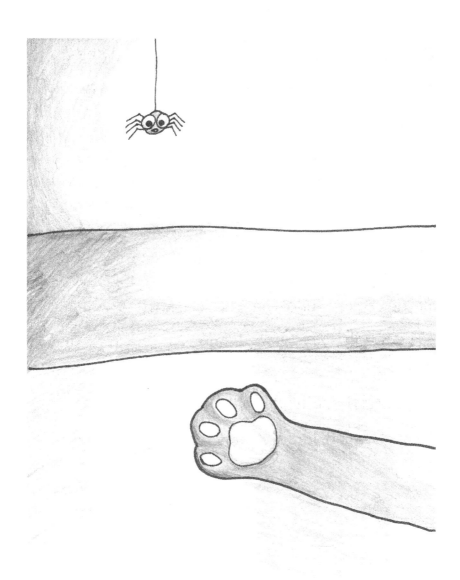

I've got so many things in my room you see.

A cat, a raven and a few other things.

Shelves are lined with my favorite books.

Bedtime stories and adventures for me.

My daddy reads them until a quarter to three.

He yawns often through the stories you see

and I make him start over if it is about a bee.

He buzzes around the story, that bee you see,

bzzz bzzz, bzzz bzzz. I hope he doesn't sting me.

For sure there is one thing that you will see,

I surely don't like a stingy bee.

Tim the cat sits idly by, waiting for daddy to make his reply.

"Good night dear princess and all will be well.

Goodnight Sir Tim, keep an eye on them all."

Daddy pats Tim's head and kisses me too

and soon the lights are out and it is just me,

Tim—and that bee.

For things lurk in the dark when the lights grow dim,

and it is good to have a cat named Tim.

Tim scurries about in the dark, I cannot see.

How in the world he is chasing that bee?

Bzzz bzzz, bzzz bzzz, it shoots right past me.

As Tim leaps on top to go after that bee.

He swats and swats next to my knee.

Swatting that bee that will not leave me be.

I wake up sweaty and scared you see.

At last it was a dream. There is no bee!

Tim sits snoring at my feet, I finally see.

His lips are so fluttery and the sound,

well...it sounds just like that bee.

Bzzz, Bzzz—Bzzz, Bzzz—his lips flutter slightly.

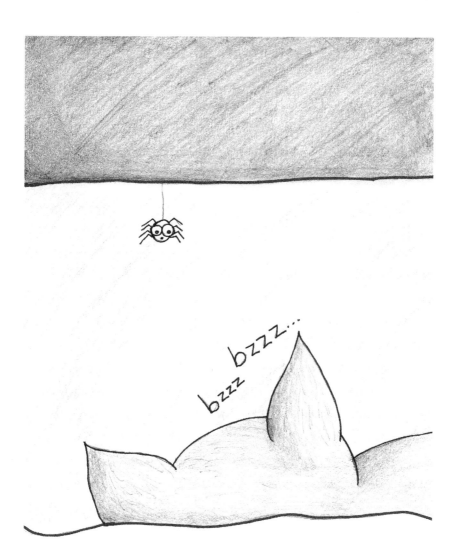

My closet door is halfway closed.

I sit and watch in the moonlight to see what will be.

My closet door is halfway closed you see, you see.

A monster may live in that closet that is closest to me.

My closet door is halfway closed you see you see.

I kick at Tim the cat to wake him up.

It is his time to stand watch while I catch some zzz's.

My closet door is halfway closed you see you see.

I am just a little girl barely past the age of three.

But closet doors halfway open make me wish I was just a bee.

At nine years old I should be bold, but closet doors half open, let in the cold.

The moon outside is bright and gold.

It fills the room, spilling its color through the window and is quite cold.

The closet door shadow moves across the floor

and I am sure that the closet door may come alive—

nah it's just a door.

Across the floor I scamper bare feet,

and fly into that door and exclaim with glee.

I've shut it smartly and fast as I can.

I'm back into bed and snug as a clam.

Daddy brought me a gold fish home from the store.

He dropped it once and it bounced on the floor.

He said "it's slippery and slimy to hold",

as he grasp it in his hand he said,

"hey he's cold."

Into the bowl swimming free,

my little gold fishy, as free as can be.

I nose up to that round piece of glass,

and give him a big eyed glance, as he swims past.

He leaps out of his bowl, as high as can be.

Jumping and splashing,

he thinks he is free.

Gold fishy, gold fishy, jump once more for me.

The raven he watches intently, planning you see.

He likes gold fishy; tastes like sushi.

But alas he misses as gold fishy splashes me,
and down to the bottom, of the deep blue sea.

Next to the pirate chest and into the sand.

Gold fishy was lucky this time, you see.

Next time he jumps high, he better look twice.

A raven is smart and a gold fishy tastes nice.

Tooth fairy, tooth fairy, I say to thee.

I've lost my front tooth, so you must come to me.

It is under my pillow—underneath me.

I wait for tooth fairy, awake to see what I can see.

Minute by minute and hour by hour.

No tooth fairy will pass, by this young flower.

Tim snores loudly, at the foot of my bed.

Bzzz bzzz, Bzzz bzzz.

Fifteen minutes later—he is sleeping next to my head.

I drift off to sleep, in my little bed.

I feel the pillow shift under my head.

I dare not open my eyes to see,

if it is the tooth fairy bringing money for me.

Back to sleep as quick as can be.

I can't wait to tell daddy that the tooth fairy visited me.

Up in a flash with the sun on my face,

searching for that five dollars under my head.

I pull out two quarters, is this change instead?

Down the hall opening the door to daddy and mummies room.

Up on their bed I stand with a broom.

I tickle dad's nose, with the broom made of straw.

To wake him up and figure out what was the guffaw.

Daddy stares at me through his foggy eyes and gruff chin.

He cannot figure out what his child is doing—

at a quarter past five, no-one should be alive.

It is too early he says with a sigh,

go back to bed—we will sort this out to which I decry.

Fifty cents is not a good sum.

For my tooth surely should be worth more.

I demand five dollars, it is what I deserve.

Daddy says goodnight princess, go back to bed,

the order makes me mad as I whack him on the head.

He forgot I was holding that broom in my hand

as I cried,

five dollars is a good sum for a tooth in my head.

Tooth fairy tooth fairy, you wait and see.

Tim and Clarence will be waiting for you

and dust bunny Fred and a raven too,

gold fishy, gold fishy, you won't escape,

the clutches of this nine year old girl and her
fairy land bedroom and a buzzing bee.

Come back to me tooth fairy and you will see,

that you owe me the difference

in coinage, times three, times three.

It is spring once again, my window open to a breeze.

My raven flies out and over to the sea.

I hear him qworking and squawking and qworking gleefully.

He makes me happy when I see him land in my tree.

Outside the window, up in that tree.

My raven jumps into my hand you see.

In his beak is a button, blue and so glittery.

My raven brings me things that I think are pretty.

Back out the window he flies with a swoosh.

Who knows when he will return,

not I—nor gold fishy.

He swooshes and qworks as he swooshes away.

Squawking and flapping wildly,

back to the ocean and the sea.

I wait in my chair by gold fishy you see.

Birds must fly it is what they do.

Not so gold fishy, it is a bowl for you.

Birds must move across the sky—

to find a worm, or string, or just to fly high.

We're off to my uncle's ranch, to see the cows on his farm.

I've packed my bag, it is under my arm.

Gold fishy, gold fishy, goodbye, take care.

I throw him a kiss, as I hug my bear.

Under the bed I yell so long, to dust bunny Fred,

and look into the corner for a spider named Clarence,

who dances above my head.

I give him a wave with the palm of my hand,

the raven and the cat left behind, in my bedroom fairy land.

Buckled into daddy's car,

I watch the house grow small

as we leave fairy land bedroom behind I forget
them all.

My nose is pressed up to the glass real hard,

blowing and huffing I draw a smiley face.

An hour later we pull into the farm yard.

Pe yew, what is that foul smell?

I see the source of the stench—

as it plops out of the back end, of the nearest
cow,

and lands in a steamy pile, next to the fence.

Plop, plop. Plop, plop.

Uncle Dale says it is profits, it hardly smells to him at all.

I think his nose is burned up—from those plopping, plop plops.

The barn full of hay is just past my reach

as I swing my feet over the fence,

to see what I can see.

I count the cows, one, two and then three.

No wait, there are four and five, that I can see.

Six and seven and a few more to the left of me.

More smell, Pe yew, pe yew,

how can this smell be something that is good for you.

I jump down from the fence and into the pasture for a closer look to see.

I have landed in mud and it is up to my knees.

It is squishy and squashy and full of flies and fleas.

Uncle Dale says mud is good for a girl like me.

Pulling hard on my rubber boot with my hand,

I tip right over and into the mud I land.

He picks me up, with one strong hand

and back on the fence where I can jump on dry land.

This mud it smells kind of funny you see, you see.

I am not sure it is mud at all,

in fact I think it is full of pee.

The cows start laughing and mooing

and I think they are laughing at me—hysterically!

Uncle Dale hoses me off, as quick as can be.

He says, "you look good, it's just fertilizer you see.

No worries, it washes off, as quick as can be,"

those laughing cows, they don't agree.

They shake their heads back and forth as they laugh at me.

A big yellow moon, just outside my window.

My dad says there is a man up there and it is made out of cheese.

I wonder how far it is from my window to the moon.

If I ran real far could I get there real soon.

Yellow moon, yellow moon, big and round.

If I kicked you hard, would you spin around.

My raven named Ned just flew through the window and said,

"It surely is a yellow moon and it is your time for bed."

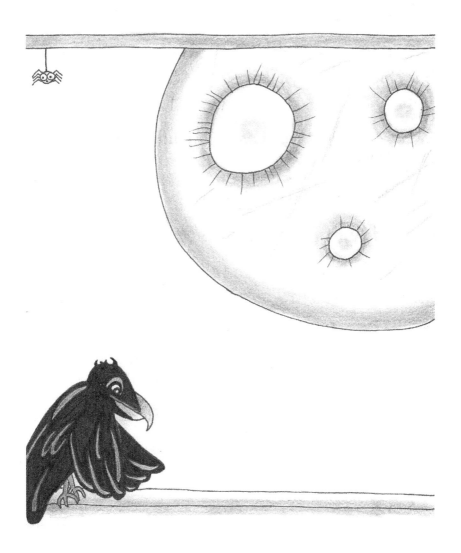

Mud puddle, mud puddle, big and round.

I fell in and now I'm dirty brown.

I stomped and I splashed, in that big round pool.

My clothes got dirty and I thought, well, this is cool.

Sloshed in my boots, up to the front door.

Walked right in and messed up mum's floor.

She looked at me with an angry grin and said, "might not want to jump into the mud puddle again."

Mud puddle, mud puddle, big and round.

I fell in and I nearly drown.

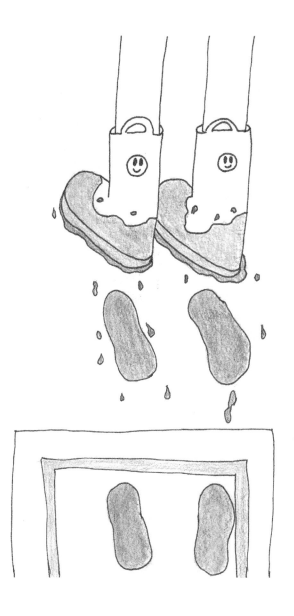

My dad's car is really neat.

He lets me drive it down the street.

He pushes the pedals, I steer the wheel.

Between his legs, I sit and I squeal.

It is big and black and out of site.

I think his car, is dy-na-mite.

Cars they go fast, when you push on the gas.

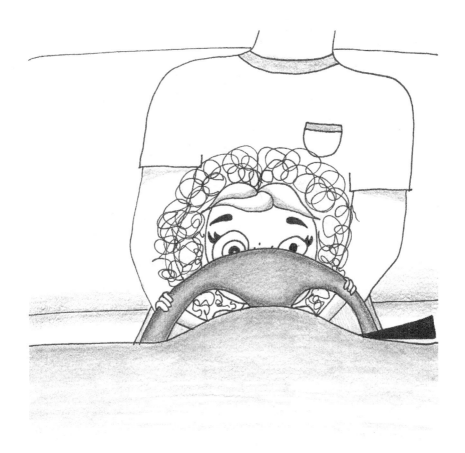

It is bubble gum Friday and I am real glad.

I missed it last Friday and it made me sad.

Three pieces for a penny, at the corner store.

If I had a nickel, I could buy a lot more.

One penny sits in my little hand,

as I skip down the street to the corner stand.

Swinging my arms as fast as can be.

Me—and my penny!

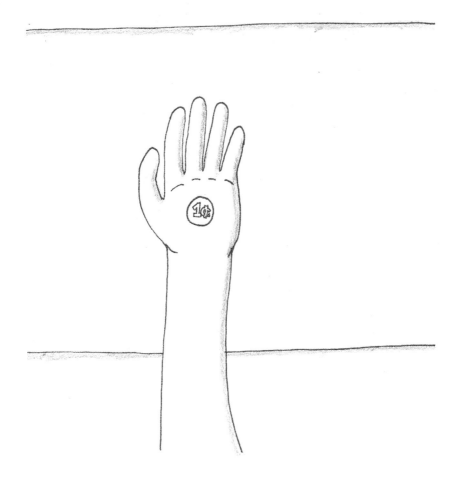

I knew what was waiting, in the store for me.

"Hey Mister store clerk," I said with a grin.

"I want this bubble gum."

He said, "I'll throw it right in."

He bagged it up, in a paper sack.

That is "one cent, young lady, how bout' that."

I open my hand and my penny is gone.

My eyes grow teary, as I search all around.

I have a plan, "It has to be on the ground."

I look up at him, with a big frown.

"I'll be right back, after I track it down."

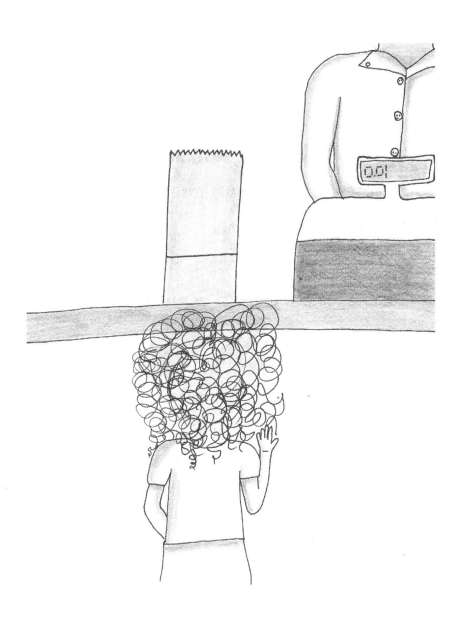

A big log truck, drove by my house the other day.

I gave him a wave, with my little hand.

He waved right back, with his big old hand.

I thought to myself, "that man is grand."

Big black tires, nearly tall as me.

Rolled right by, picking up the leaves.

I kicked and frolicked, as the leaves blew around.

It was the funnest game in my town.

Neighborhood kids stand next to the street you see.

To see if the big truck, will pass right by me.

I like spaghetti, in my bowl.

I slurp it up, even though it is cold.

Twist it, turn it, on my fork.

Pop it into my mouth, with my fork.

Spaghetti, spaghetti, I yell to my mum,

It tastes good, yum—yum—yum.

Clarence bounces in the web up high,

over my head and above my bed.

He hangs from the ceiling, as he scurries about,

looking for a fly, as it buzzes by,

that spider is crafty, as you will see—

buzzing by my face, that fly passes by me.

I swat at him twice and my raven takes note.

A fly would be tasty—for a raven you see,

there is nothing better, except maybe a worm you see.

Worms are squishy and squirmy and squishy to me,

they are slimy to the touch and slither in my palm,

when gold fishy eats one, he swallows it and it makes me frown.

The raven, the fly, they pass right by,

buzzing and flapping, the battle goes down,

around and around, the raven chases him down.

With a snap of his beak, he swallows that fly
down.

Out of my sheets,

JUMPING off my bed.

I flew down the stairs

and nearly landed on my head.

The door-bell had rang

as it jangled and clanged.

The knocking it started

and I was startled.

Peering out of the mail slot,

in the middle of our front door,

the blue trousers and legs I saw,

told me more.

I had waited and waited for weeks you see,

for that mailman, and friend, to bring a package
for me.

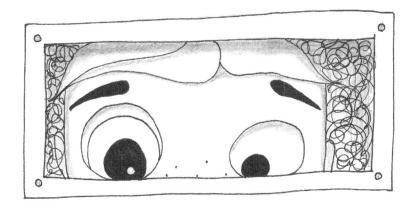

I flung the door open as fast as could be

and scared mister mailman, as he ran up the tree.

He stared down at me, with a big ol' grin, with

his fluffy brown mustache, tweaking again.

The box in his hands, was big and brown and

the words on the outside said,

"THIS SIDE/UPSIDE DOWN."

I jumped up and down with joy and glee.

I could not wait, to see what the mailman had brought for me.

Sign here young lady, and it is all yours.

He handed me the board and paper where I signed R.J, as I sat on the floor—upstairs you could hear Tim snore.

Bzzz bzzz. Bzzz bzzz.

Grabbing that box as fast as I could, I cleared five stairs as I flew up to my room. Ripping and tearing, to open it up. I sliced my hand and got a paper cut. Into mum's room, sniffing you see, the tears were flowing, free-fully. Mum took one look and said, "I know what to do, stay right there," as she looked for some glue. It said it was super and I am not quite sure, but that blood stopped leaking and it stung a bit too.

Back to the box, the top nearly ripped off, my finger throbbed, as I dug right in. Pushing and pulling, I grabbed what I could and nearly fell in.

The squishy surprise came up with a tug, a brand new fluffy bear with matching rug. I think I nearly squeezed the life out of him, as he grunted and snorted and smiled at his new friend. Thank you mister mailman for bringing Hermann to me. I'm glad my bear traveled so well. It must be tough to sit at the bottom of a box, all alone in the cold and dark, as the truck left the docks.

My fairy land bedroom is a neat place to be,

with a gold fishy and a dust bunny named Fred.

My fairy land bedroom and a spider over head.

A raven named Ned, who ate that fly instead,

Tim the cat and the stuffed bear next to me.

How can the fairy land bedroom not be the
place for me!

Tooth fairy you better come visit me soon,

a tooth feels loose and it's nearly a full moon.

Where a spider, a raven and a gold fishy live
with me.

In the fairy land bedroom with dust bunny
Fred.

Where Tim the cat sleeps next to my head.
Bzzz bzzz. Bzzz bzzz.

END

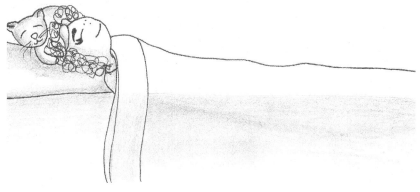

BRIELLE BARTEL, illustrator and musician, lives in the Pacific Northwest with her husband, their little girl, a dog and two cats. She enjoys doing all kinds of art with her daughter. She also volunteers at her daughter's school, enjoys writing songs with her husband and cooking delicious meals.